THE URBANA FREE LIBRARY
3 1230 00907 7732

David Chelsea's
SNOW ANGEL
TM

D1416906

Foreword

by Rebecca Celsi

Meet Snow Angel, the tweenage superheroine unlike any other you've met. There are no bad guys to face here, no plots to be foiled, just the inane senselessness of the human race and the small crimes that must be corrected. The character of Snow Angel is stubborn and hot tempered. She often feels unappreciated and cares deeply about the things she feels are important—things like littering, incorrect table settings, and filching from penny dishes. Her powers are of immense magnitude, yet her aspirations are pitifully modest. She can alter the very motion of the Earth—the very delicate equations and cosmic balances that keep all life in existence—in order to play in the snow. She may even come closer to destroying the Earth than improving it in any meaningful way, but all Snow Angel really wants is a clean neighborhood and a peaceful game of Settlers of Catan.

When the first *Snow Angel* installment came to my attention in 2007, it did so fresh from the creator's hands. It was pored over by my brother and me in the same manner as my father's other 24-hour comics: crowded around the kitchen table while Dad took a much-needed nap upstairs.

I was seven years old and enjoying this installment more than usual. The other 24-hour comics I'd read tended to go over my head, as they were steeped in oddball references, sexual innuendo, and a deep-seated, sleepless incomprehensibility that meandered through the plot. But that morning, I found the reveal of the previous night's scribbling fascinating—for it conveyed a tale that was more understandable and relatable, and seemed to feature a familiar face.

I cannot deny that the character of Snow Angel within the following pages is based on me—much as her brother, Aidan, is based on my brother, Ben. It is very well to be seven and wear pigtails and not want to clean one's room, but to watch this character have adventures and exploits of her own while growing up has been an odd experience. It serves as a reminder of a simpler time, when the only important things were days at the beach, board games, and trick-or-treating. At fifteen, though I'm very different from the part of me that inspired Angel, I can finally appreciate the wit and originality of the story. I leap to read each page as it is inked, sitting cross-legged in Dad's studio, reveling in the unexpected twists and turns of Angel's life.

Enjoy the quirky little world you're about to dive into—I've lived it, he's drawn it, and now all the action is all together for the first time.

—**Rebecca Celsi**
Portland, Oregon
September 2015

Rebecca Celsi is the daughter of David Chelsea.
The name thing is kind of complicated.

Contents

All stories written and drawn by
David Chelsea
unless otherwise noted

Colors by
David Chelsea
and **Jacob Mercy**

Foreword by
Rebecca Celsi

DARK HORSE BOOKS

President and Publisher
Mike Richardson

Editor
Philip R. Simon

Designer
Ethan Kimberling

Digital Art Technician
Christianne Goudreau

Published by Dark Horse Books
A division of Dark Horse Comics, Inc.
10956 SE Main Street
Milwaukie, OR 97222

DarkHorse.com
DChelsea.com

To find a comics shop in your area, call the Comic Shop Locator Service toll-free at 1-888-266-4226.

The short story "Snow Angel" appeared in *Dark Horse Presents* Volume 2, #1–#3 (2011), and in the *Snow Angel* one-shot comic special (2013). "Snow Angel Halloween" appeared in *Dark Horse Presents* Volume 3, #15 (2015).

First edition: April 2016
ISBN 978-1-61655-940-3

1 3 5 7 9 10 8 6 4 2

Printed in China

Story & Art by David Chelsea

THANK YOU, SNOW ANGEL!!

AND JUST WHERE HAVE YOU BEEN?

YOUR FATHER AND I HAVE BEEN WORRIED SICK!! WE DIDN'T KNOW IF YOU WERE ALIVE OR DEAD!

HONESTLY, I THOUGHT YOU'D LEARNED YOUR LESSON THE TIME YOU DISAPPEARED AT TIMBERLINE LODGE AND WE HAD TO CALL OUT THE–

HOLD ON– DID YOU TURN INTO SNOW ANGEL AGAIN?

WELL–?

MA, I KNOW I PROMISED I WOULDN'T TURN INTO SNOW ANGEL BUT THAT KID STOLE MR. PURVIS'S BIKE AND...

...HE WOULD'VE GOTTEN AWAY WITH IT, TOO – IF IT HADN'T BEEN FOR SNOW ANGEL!

WE'VE BEEN THROUGH THIS A MILLION TIMES! YOU CAN'T TURN INTO SNOW ANGEL WITHOUT A GROWNUP AROUND! IT'S TOO DANGEROUS! YOU COULD BREAK YOUR ARM!

WELL, NEVER MIND – IT'S NOT GOING TO MATTER AT ALL SOON – WE WERE GOING TO TELL YOU AFTER YOUR BIRTHDAY BUT YOU MIGHT AS WELL KNOW IT NOW. YOUR FATHER IS STARTING A NEW JOB IN TUCSON!
RING!

HA HA! IT NEVER SNOWS THERE!

WHAT'D I SAY?
! !

THAT WAS ED PURVIS, HE JUST WANTED TO THANK—
NOT NOW!

SLAM!

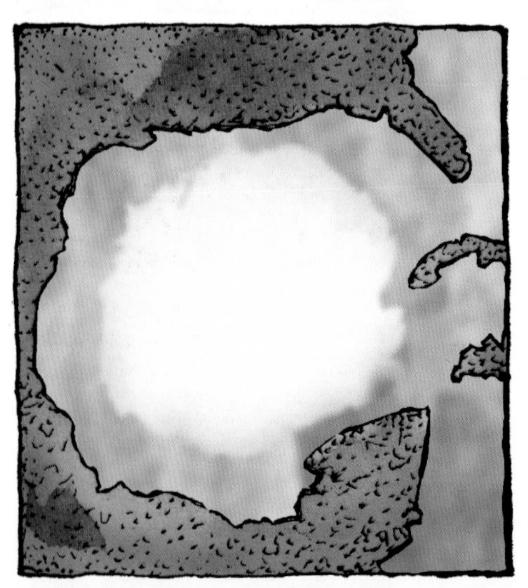

SP

TUG TIGHTLY REPORTING ON THE UNPRECEDENTED SHIFT IN THE EARTH'S POLAR AXIS!
POLAR CRISIS

ROSE SHARPLEY REPORTING FROM THE SHORES OF ANTARCTICA.

MIDAS WELBY LIVE FROM THE NEW SOUTH POLE, SOMEWHERE IN THE INDIAN OCEAN.
SP

YES, AND SOON AS WE CAN, WE'LL BE MOVING THE WHOLE OPERATION TO THE GULF OF MEXICO
YES!

OLIVE TAPENADE HERE IN TUCSON, ARIZONA, WHERE FOR THE FIRST TIME IN LIVING MEMORY, CHILDREN ARE PLAYING IN THE SNOW!

EVEN MAKING SNOW ANGELS!
YOU SEE— TUCSON WON'T BE SO BAD!

HEY— HOLD ON A MINUTE!

HONEY— DID YOU DO SOMETHING TO THE POLES?

SOMETHING LIKE WHAT, MOM?

OH— NEVER MIND.

SO, HOW'S IT GOIN', FALCON?
NOT BAD, NOT BAD AT ALL, SNOWMAN.

SO, OK, I'VE GOT THIS IDEA FOR A GREAT PRODUCT. DO YOU WANT TO HEAR ABOUT IT?
WHY, YES I DO, SNOWMAN.

GGRRR!!..

WHAT WAS THAT?
I THINK IT SOUNDED LIKE THE ANGRIEST DOG IN THE WORLD.

SO YOU WERE GOING TO TELL ME ABOUT YOUR GREAT IDEA.
RIGHT!

OK, YOU REMEMBER WHO WILLIAM HENRY HARRISON WAS, RIGHT?
UH — REFRESH MY MEMORY.

WILLIAM HENRY HARRISON
(1773 – 1841)
NINTH PRESIDENT OF
THE UNITED STATES
(1841)

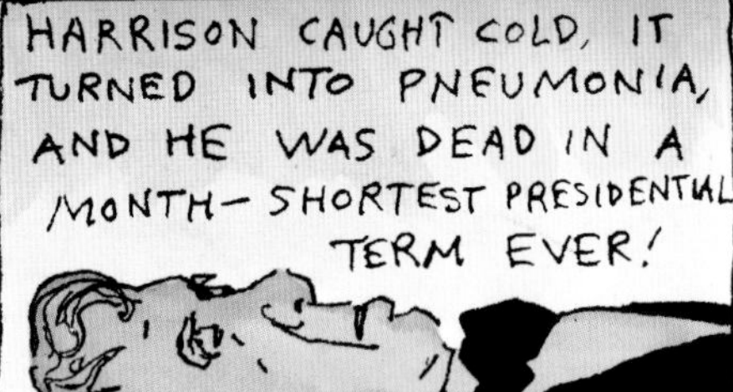

GENIUS.
IT COULD PLAY HARRISON'S CAMPAIGN SONG— "TIPPECANOE AND TYLER TOO"—

SO— ARE YOU FEELING COLD AT ALL?
NO, NOT REALLY— YOU?

YEAH, I KIND OF AM.
WELL, MAYBE YOU SHOULD GO INSIDE.

YEAH, I THINK I WILL.

SEE YA!

I...GOTTA GO—
PLAY NICE, DEAR.

WHUMP!

WHAT TH-?

JAYWALKING IS SELFISH AND DANGEROUS - SO DON'T DO IT! WHAT WOULD YOUR MOTHER THINK?
YOU'RE RIGHT!

THANK YOU, SNOW ANGEL!

COME ON, KIDS—
SING ALONG WITH THE SNOW ANGEL SONG—JUST FOLLOW THE BOUNCING SNOWBALL!

THERE'S A GIRL WHO'S ALWAYS IN THE KNOW—
SNOW ANGEL!

SHE COMES FROM A WORLD THAT'S MADE OF SNOW—

IF YOUR KITTEN'S CAUGHT UP A TREE—

YOU'RE LOCKED OUT AND YOU CAN'T FIND THE KEY—

GIVE A CALL AND SHE'LL KNOW WHERE TO GO—
SNOW ANGEL!

AND DON'T FORGET TO LOOK FOR YOUR FREE WILLIAM HENRY HARRISON SNOW GLOBE!
'TWILL ONLY HELP TO SPEED THE BALL FOR TIPPECANOE AND TYLER TOO
INSIDE SPECIALLY MARKED PACKAGES OF
SNOW ANGEL BRAND SNO-CUBES
SNOW ANGEL SNO-CUBE
THE CUBES GUARANTEED TO MAKE ANY DRINK TASTE LIKE SNOW!
IN YOUR GROCER'S FREEZER!
BINGO

YOU'LL HAVE A BRAIN FREEZE WHEN YOU SEE THE TERRORS THAT FACE SNOW ANGEL IN HER NEXT COMIC!

NOISY DOGS!
YELP
YELP
YELP
YELP

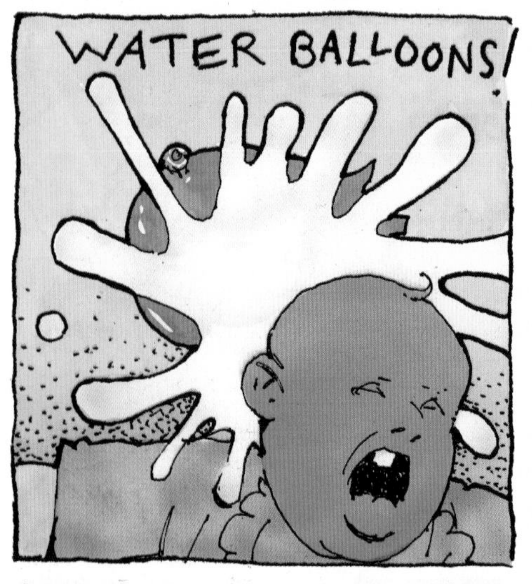
WATER BALLOONS!

STICKY GUM!

SMOKING IN CHURCH!

THE FORECAST IS FOR HEAVY WEATHER AND HIGH PRESSURE IN THE NEXT
SNOW ANGEL!

Story & Art by David Chelsea | Colors by Jacob Mercy

COAST
60
MILES

DO NOT REMOVE TIDE POOL ANIMALS!

HI.

YOU MAKING A SAND CASTLE?
YEAH.

CAN I HELP?
SURE.

MY NAME'S ALBANY. WHAT'S YOURS?
ANGEL.

THIS IS BORING. CAN WE DO SOMETHING DIFFERENT?
HOW ABOUT WE BUILD A FORT?

SO, ARE YOU SNOW ANGEL?
YEAH. HOW'D YOU KNOW?

WELL, YOUR NAME'S ANGEL, FOR ONE THING—
YEAH, THERE IS THAT—

AND YOUR BROTHER OVER THERE IS WEARING A SNOW ANGEL T-SHIRT.

DO YOU THINK I COULD GET A SHIRT LIKE THAT?
LET'S ASK MY BROTHER!

AIDAN, THIS IS MY FRIEND ALBANY THAT I JUST MET. CAN SHE HAVE YOUR SHIRT?
NO WAY! GET REAL!

WE'LL LET YOU HELP US BUILD A FORT!
PLEASE? I'M A REALLY BIG FAN!
IT'S TOO COLD! GET YOUR OWN SHIRT!

MEANIE!

CAN YOU TURN INTO SNOW ANGEL ANYTIME YOU WANT TO?
NO, ONLY WHEN THERE'S SNOW AROUND.

HEY, YOU KNOW WHAT- I'M PRETTY SURE I PACKED A SHIRT IN MY SUITCASE. I COULD GO LOOK FOR IT.

YOU WAIT HERE. I'LL BE RIGHT BACK.

RIIIING!!

HELLO-YES, THIS IS- WHO'S CALLING? OH, HELLO, GOVERNOR- WHY ARE YOU CALLING ME?
HEY, MOM, HAVE YOU SEEN MY SNOW ANGEL T-SHIRT?

THE SUGAR CUBE ROBOTS ARE ATTACKING! SNOW ANGEL IS OUR ONLY HOPE!!

ANGEL, WOULD YOU BE QUIET? I'M SORRY, GOVERNOR, YOU'RE BREAKING UP- COULD YOU SAY THAT AGAIN?

THE SUGAR CUBE ROBOTS ARE ATTACKING! SNOW ANGEL IS OUR ONLY HOPE!!

I'D LIKE TO HELP YOU, GOVERNOR- BUT IT'S THE MIDDLE OF AUGUST!
THAT'S WHY I'M SENDING A HELICOPTER!!

THE SUGAR CUBE ROBOTS ARE ATTACKING THE CITY! I'M HERE TO TAKE YOU AND YOUR DAUGHTER TO MOUNT HOOD!
OH, I GET IT! SO I CAN TURN INTO SNOW ANGEL!

MA'AM, WOULD YOU AND YOUR DAUGHTER PLEASE STEP INSIDE-
JUST A MOMENT- I HAVE TO GO GET MY SON!

I'M SORRY- THERE'S ONLY ROOM FOR TWO PASSENGERS IN THE HELICOPTER.
WELL, I'M NOT GOING TO LEAVE MY SON UNSUPERVISED!

IT'S OK, MOM- I'LL GO BY MYSELF!
THAT WON'T WORK EITHER- ANYONE UNDER TWELVE NEEDS TO RIDE WITH A PARENT.
IT WOULD BE DIFFERENT IF MY HUSBAND WERE HERE, BUT HE HAD TO STAY BEHIND TO WORK ON OUR TAXES- SEE, WE DIDN'T GET AROUND TO FILING IN APRIL, AND-
LET ME KNOW WHEN YOU GET THIS STRAIGHTENED OUT-

SORRY- I COULDN'T FIND THE SHIRT.
THAT'S OK-
WE'RE PUTTING AN ANNEX ON THE FORT.

MOM'S CALLING. SHE SAYS COME ON BACK TO THE HOUSE.

WHAT'S THAT?
WE COMPROMISED. THE GOVERNOR SENT A SNOW MAKER.

COOL.
TRY IT OUT!

BRRR! IT'S C-COLD!!

I WISH YOU COULD BE HERE TO SEE THIS, PEOPLE! SNOW ANGEL IS DEMOLISHING THE SUGAR CUBE ROBOTS, LITERALLY CAGING THEM IN A WEB OF ICE!
5

THANK YOU, SNOW ANGEL!

OH, HI, SNOW ANGEL!
HI, DAD! I'M JUST COMING IN TO GET A T-SHIRT!

HOW'S EVERYTHING AT THE BEACH?
OH, IT'S GREAT! TOO BAD YOU HAVE TO WORK.

HI- I GOT THE SHIRT- WHERE'S ALBANY?
SHE HAD TO GO IN FOR DINNER- SHE SAID SHE MIGHT BE BACK TOMORROW.

HEY- I SAVED THE CITY FROM THE SUGAR CUBE ROBOTS!
YEAH, I SAW- IT WAS ON THE NEWS.
HERE - WANNA WATCH?

IT'S RAINING!
GOOD THING WE BUILT THIS FORT.

End

Story & Art by David Chelsea | Colors by Jacob Mercy

THIS IS A VERY ELABORATE COSTUME, SO YOU CAN'T BE SNEAKING OFF AND TURNING INTO SNOW ANGEL WHILE YOU'RE WEARING IT!

SO, WHAT DO I DO ABOUT THAT, MOM?

THESE PILLS ARE SUPPOSED TO SUPPRESS YOUR VOICES.
THEY'RE NOT VOICES EXACTLY, MOM. MORE LIKE—

JUST TAKE ONE—

I DON'T FEEL ANYTHING—
WE HAVE TO TEST IT!

HOW DO WE DO THAT?
FIRST, I SNEAK BEHIND YOU—

NOW, I DO SOMETHING NAUGHTY—
I KNOW YOU'RE RAIDING THE COOKIE JAR!

HOW CAN YOU TELL?
WHAT ELSE IS BEHIND ME?

WELL, I HAVE TO GO ELSEWHERE—

YELL IF YOU PICK UP ANY VIBRATIONS!

I'M BACK! NO VIBRATIONS?
NOTHING.

HERE'S YOUR DIARY!
MOM!!

THANKS FOR CARRYING MY BUCKET, AIDAN.

HMM- I SENSE A PATTERN HERE.
I GUESS I SHOULD BE FLATTERED.

HELP! HELP!

WHICH ONE OF YOU IS SNOW ANGEL?
I AM SNOW ANGEL!
NO, I AM SNOW ANGEL!
I AM SNOW ANGEL!

ACTUALLY, I AM SNOW ANGEL, BUT I'M KIND OF OFF DUTY FOR THE NIGHT. WHAT'S THE PROBLEM?
SOME KIDS ARE THROWING EGGS AT MY HOUSE!

CAN'T YOU JUST CHASE 'EM OFF?
THEY'RE BIG KIDS! TEENAGERS!

WHY ARE THEY THROWING EGGS AT YOUR HOUSE?
BECAUSE I WOULDN'T GIVE THEM ANY CANDY!

WELL, THEN, THEY'RE ENTIRELY WITHIN THEIR RIGHTS.
YEAH, IT'S TRICK OR TREAT. YOU WOULDN'T TREAT THEM. THAT'S THEIR TRICK.
NOW, YOU CAN OPT OUT BY NOT PUTTING ANY DECORATIONS UP AND LEAVING YOUR PORCH LIGHT OFF.
I WOULDN'T DO THAT! IT'S NOT SAFE!

I'M SORRY, I CAN'T HELP YOU. HAVE YOU TRIED CALLING 911?
OF COURSE! I'VE BEEN ON HOLD FOR TWENTY MINUTES!

YEAH, HALLOWEEN. NOT THE BEST TIME TO CALL.
IT SAYS HERE YOU CAN WASH EGGS OFF YOUR HOUSE WITH WARM WATER!

HELP! SNOW ANGEL! BAD KIDS ARE THROWING ROCKS AT MY CAT!
THEY'RE THROWING ROCKS AT EBONY?

BLACK CATS. PEOPLE REALLY SHOULDN'T LET THEM OUT ON HALLOWEEN!
WELL, THAT'S JUST HEINOUS! HELP ME GET THIS COSTUME OFF, AIDAN!

NOW, I COULD ENCASE THOSE BAD KIDS IN ICE... OR GIVE THEM BAD FROSTBITE SO THEY CAN'T LIFT THOSE ROCKS, OR BUILD A WALL OF SNOW TO PROTECT THE HOUSE...
BUT I PROBABLY WON'T HAVE TO DO ANY OF THAT--

WHAP!
POW!

OOOWOO!! LEAVE THAT CAT ALONE!!

LOOK! IN THE SKY! IT'S A GHOST!
IT'S AN ANGEL!
IT'S A GHOST ANGEL!

THAT'S RIIIIGHT!! I'M A GHOOOOOST ANGEL!

BEGONE! THIS IS YOUR LAAAST WARNING!!
LEMME OUTTA HERE!
SHE'S GAINING ON US!
WAIT FOR ME!

POOR LITTLE GUY - LET'S PUT YOU BACK INSIDE! THIS IS NO NIGHT FOR A CAT TO BE OUT!

HI, I'M BACK!
HI, ANGEL. AREN'T YOU GOING TO CHANGE BACK?

NO, I'M FINE WITH BEING SNOW ANGEL ANOTHER YEAR– BESIDES, THIS HEADLESS-MAN COSTUME WILL LOOK JUST AS COOL LYING HERE IN THE SNOW!

COME ON, KIDS! LET'S GO TRICK-OR-TREATING!

I AM SNOW ANGEL!
NO, I AM SNOW ANGEL!
YOU'RE BOTH WRONG! I AM SNOW ANGEL!
WE ARE ALL SNOW ANGEL!

LISTEN TO SNOW ANGEL:
GIVE GENEROUSLY AT HALLOWEEN, BUT IF FOR SOME REASON YOU CAN'T, SIGNAL BY LEAVING YOUR PORCH LIGHT OFF, AND NOT PUTTING UP ANY DECORATIONS! AND LEAVE YOUR CAT IN AT NIGHT– THERE ARE SOME MEAN PEOPLE OUT THERE!

Story & Art by David Chelsea | Colors by Jacob Mercy

CHOCOLATE

R!!!NG!!!

HEY, ANGEL— DO YOU WANT TO COME OVER THIS AFTERNOON AND PLAY GAMES?
SURE, VIOLET, AS LONG AS IT'S NOT TWISTER!

OK, TWO WHEATS ARE AN ORE, AND TWO MORE WHEATS ARE WHEATS, AND TWO MORE ORES ARE ORES, AND I'M BUYING A CITY!

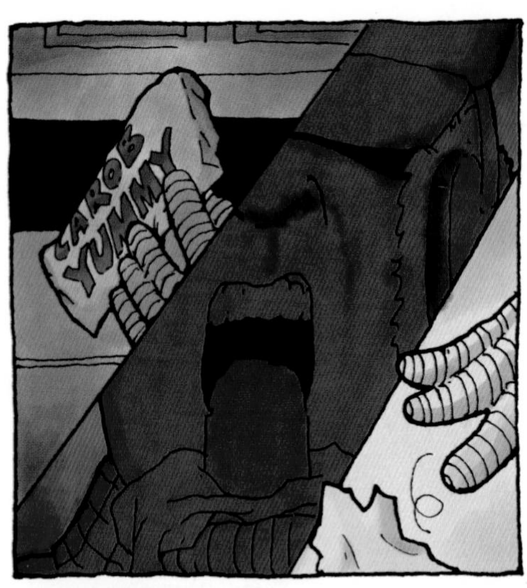
CAROB YUMMY

UH- CAN EVERYONE EXCUSE ME FOR A MINUTE?

LITTER MUCH?

ABOUT TIME - IT'S YOUR TURN!

SO - HOW'D YOU LIKE THE SNOW, ANGEL?

ALL RIGHT, I'M PLAYING A KNIGHT CARD - I WANT WHEAT AND SHEEP!
UHH-

'SCUZE ME!

WHAT WAS IT THIS TIME—
SOMEBODY LOSE A MITTEN?
WE WENT AHEAD AND PLAYED YOUR TURN— YOU NOW OWN THE WOOD DOCK!

OK-SO, I'M PLAYING A ROAD-BUILDING CARD, AND THAT GIVES ME LONGEST ROAD- PLUS, THE-
ANGEL?

ANGEL- SHE'S ABOUT TO WIN THE GAME ANYWAY, SO JUST GO!!

KRRRRK!!

KRASH!

WOW!!
MISSED THE HOUSE BY THAT MUCH!
THANK YOU, SNOW ANGEL!

NO, I'M JUST ANGEL— I MEAN, A MINUTE AGO I WAS, BUT—
WHATEVER YOU CALL YOURSELF, THANK YOU!

SO, WHAT DO YOU WANT TO DO NOW, ANGEL?
YOU UP FOR ANOTHER GAME?

SOMEBODY UNPLUG ANGEL— IT'S HER TURN!

Story & Art by David Chelsea | Colors by Jacob Mercy

WELL, I WAS GOING TO SURPRISE YOU WITH IT FOR YOUR BIRTHDAY, BUT- LOOK, I DESIGNED A SNOW ANGEL FIGURINE IN MY 3-D MODELING PROGRAM AND PRINTED IT OUT ON MY MAKERBOT!

WHY DOES IT HAVE A HOLE IN ITS STOMACH?

YOU TAKE AN ICE CUBE, DROP IT INSIDE THE HEAD, PUSH DOWN THE HALO, TURN THE CRANK, AND SNOW COMES OUT!

THESE THINGS ARE GOING TO SELL LIKE HOTCAKES!

LIKE HOTCAKES, I THINK THEY'D BE BETTER WITH A BIT OF MAPLE SYRUP.

THIS IS A COMICS CONVENTION, RIGHT? AREN'T PEOPLE GOING TO EXPECT US TO SELL COMIC BOOKS?

YEAH, BUT I CAN'T DRAW THAT WELL, AND NEITHER CAN YOU.

MAYBE WE DON'T NEED TO-

OFFICER, HELP! I CAN'T GET THIS STICKY GUM OUT OF MY HAIR!
WHAT CAN I DO? I'M ONLY A POLICEMAN! THIS IS A JOB FOR-
SNOW ANGEL!!

AIDAN, YOU'RE GOING TO EDIT OUT THE YELLOW SPOTS, RIGHT?
OF COURSE!

GREAT STUFF, ANGEL, BUT MORE... INTENSITY!!

SNOW ANGEL!!
HAVE NO FEAR! A BLAST OF MY MIGHTY FREEZE BREATH WILL HAVE THAT GUM OUT OF YOUR HAIR IN NO TIME!!

SEE? IT FREEZES HARD, THEN COMES OUT EASILY!

THANK YOU, SNOW ANGEL!!

NICE WORK, EVERYBODY! NOW ALL I HAVE TO DO IS E-MAIL THE IMAGES TO MY COMPUTER, ADD A COMIC BOOK FILTER IN PHOTOSHOP, ADD PANELS AND BALLOONS IN INDESIGN, PRINT IT OUT, AND WE'VE GOT OURSELVES A COMIC BOOK!

WHAT DO YOU THINK, ANGEL?
WOW!
SNOW angel

SO, I JUST READ ON THE CON WEBSITE THAT OUR TABLE IS HALF OFF IF THERE'S SOMEONE IN COSTUME SITTING AT IT....
I CAN'T TURN INTO SNOW ANGEL FOR THE CON, AIDAN. ALL THE SNOW HAS MELTED!

SNOW angel
SNOW ANGEL ENTERPRISES

SNOW ANGEL, HUH? MIND IF I LOOK AT YOUR COMIC?
GO RIGHT AHEAD.
SNOW ANGEL ENTERPRISES

HMM– A KID SUPERHERO WITH MR. FREEZE POWERS– VERY UNUSUAL. NICE IRONIC USE OF COMIC SANS.
NOT ONLY THAT, BUT SNOW ANGEL ACTUALLY EXISTS IN THE REAL WORLD!
SNOW angel

I SEE... AND I TAKE IT YOU ARE SNOW ANGEL?
NO, I AM. IT'S COMPLICATED.

SO, YOU CAN JUST TURN INTO A SUPERHERO WHENEVER YOU FEEL LIKE IT?
NO, THERE HAS TO BE SNOW AROUND.

PITY. I WOULD LIKE TO HAVE SEEN IT. AND WHAT'S THIS?
SNOW ANGEL SNOW CONE MAKER. WANT A SAMPLE?

VERY REFRESHING– I'D TOTALLY BUY ONE IF I HAD ANY MONEY!
HOW COME YOU DON'T HAVE ANY MONEY?

IT'S THIS DARN COSTUME! NO ROOM FOR A WALLET!
SO HOW MUCH HAVE WE MADE SO FAR?
FOUR DOLLARS AND EIGHTY-SEVEN CENTS.

NOT EXACTLY LIVING UP TO EXPECTATIONS HERE—
I DON'T GET IT! THE GUY AT THAT TABLE IS DOING GREAT BUSINESS!

SHINY OBJECTS

MIND IF I WANDER AROUND THE HALL A BIT?
THIS SEEMS LIKE A PERFECT TIME.

OH WOW! THERE'S MY FAVORITE MANGA ARTIST, TIRAMISU INKAWASHI!

OOH— I DON'T WANT TO WAIT IN THAT LINE, THOUGH...
TIRAMISU INKAWASHI

WHAT A GYP! TIRAMISU INKAWASHI DIDN'T EVEN SIGN MY COMIC — SHE JUST DREW THIS LITTLE CARTOON ON IT!

OH, BUT TIRAMISU INKAWASHI NEVER SIGNS HER NAME - SHE FEELS THAT IT IS NOT HUMBLE AND NOT IN HARMONY WITH THE UNIVERSE TO SIGN A BOOK BELONGING TO ANOTHER!

THE FIGURE SHE DRAWS IN YOUR BOOK REFLECTS YOUR SPIRIT AS SHE SEES IT - YOURS IS SOME KIND OF CHIPMUNK WITH BAT WINGS - I THINK IT MEANS YOU ARE SMALL YET BRAVE.

I'M A BIG FAN, CAN YOU TELL?

STILL NO BUSINESS - I GUESS THERE'S NO REASON NOT TO TAKE A LUNCH BREAK -

EXCUSE ME - IS THAT A VOODOO DONUTS BOX?
WHY, YES, IT IS.

ARE YOU GOING TO EAT THAT CHOCOLATE ONE WITH THE COCONUT SHAVINGS?
I WAS PLANNING TO, YES.

THEY'RE OUT OF DONUTS AT THE SNACK BAR, AND I WAS WONDERING IF I COULD MAYBE HAVE HALF-
FIVE BUCKS.

EXCUSE ME?
EIGHT FOR THE WHOLE THING— OH, AND YOU HAVE TO BUY A COMIC.

I DON'T CARE FOR YOUR TONE.
I'M TAKING A BITE IN TEN, NINE...

ALL RIGHT! I'LL TAKE THE WHOLE DONUT AND AN ISSUE OF "SNOW ANGEL"!
IT'S A PLEASURE DOING BUSINESS WITH A MAN OF YOUR EXCELLENT TASTE!

THAT SETTLES IT! TOMORROW I'M BRINGING MORE SNACKS!
THE FUTURE OF COMICS!
SNOW ANGEL ENTERPRISES
GARLIC PRESS

COSPLAY MAN THUNDERCON
THE NEXT BIG THING IN COMICS
SNACKS
HMM... THERE SURE ARE A LOT OF PEOPLE IN SUGAR CUBE ROBOT COSTUMES AT THIS CONVENTION!
THE CUTTING EDGE OF COMICS

HEY! SUGAR CUBE ROBOT! HOW COME THERE'S SO MANY OF YOU AROUND?
WE'RE SECURITY!

THAT DOESN'T MAKE ANY SENSE - THE SUGAR CUBE ROBOTS ARE BAD GUYS!

HMM - MAYBE I'LL LOOK AT SOME POSTERS -

HOLD ON - THERE'S SOMETHING WRONG HERE!

I HAVE A QUESTION ABOUT THIS POSTER—
BEAUTIFUL, ISN'T IT? SIGNED AND NUMBERED BY TIRAMISU INKAWASHI HERSELF!
THAT'S JUST IT— TIRAMISU INKAWASHI NEVER SIGNS HER NAME TO ANYTHING!
WHAT'S A LITTLE GIRL LIKE YOU KNOW ABOUT MANGA?

WHY, I SAW INKAWASHI SIGN IT MYSELF!
I KNOW SHE'S AT THE CON — WE COULD ASK HER TO AUTHENTICATE IT!
SHE'S ON TO US, KARL! LET'S PACK UP AND BEAT IT!

THIS IS A JOB FOR— THE SUGAR CUBE ROBOTS!
PURLOINED PRODUCTIONS
HEY, SECURITY! THERE'S A COUPLE HERE SELLING PIRATED TIRAMISU INKAWASHI PRINTS!
OH NO! WE MUST STOP THEM!

CALLING ALL ROBOTS! WE HAVE A PRINT PIRATE EMERGENCY!

AFTER THEM! THEY WENT THAT WAY!

KRASH!

MAN! IT IS IMPOSSIBLE TO RUN IN THESE THINGS!

THEY'RE GETTING AWAY! THIS IS A JOB FOR SNOW ANGEL!

BUT, BUT... WHAT CAN I DO? THERE'S NO SNOW AROUND!

WAIT A MINUTE!!

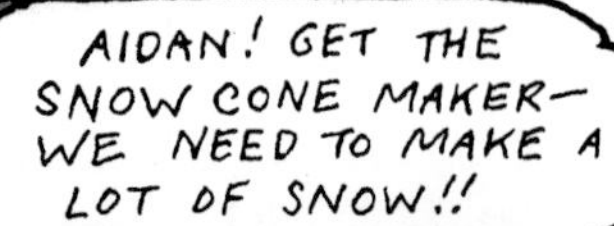
AIDAN! GET THE SNOW CONE MAKER– WE NEED TO MAKE A LOT OF SNOW!!

WELL, THAT'S KIND OF DIFFICULT– THE ICE IN THE BUCKET'S PRETTY MUCH MELTED–

I'LL GO GET MORE FROM THE ICE MACHINE– YOU GET SOME PEOPLE TOGETHER– WE'LL NEED TO USE EVERY ONE OF THOSE SNOW CONE MAKERS!
KITTY KLEEN

ICE
KITTY KLEEN

ALL RIGHT, EVERYBODY, START GRINDING! I'LL GO GET MORE ICE!!

IT HAS TO WORK!
IT HAS TO!

MORE SNOW!!

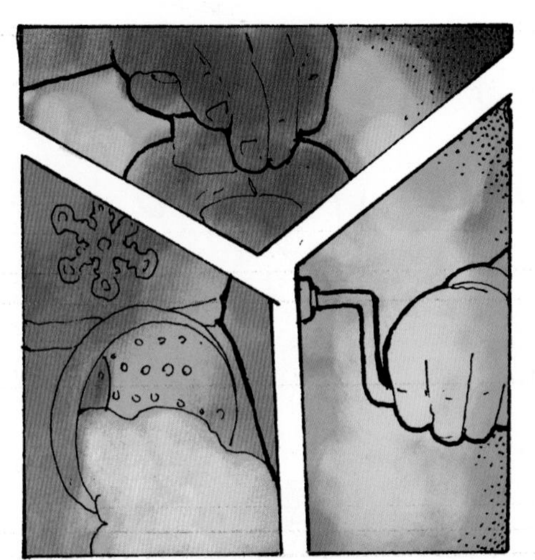

COMING THROUGH!
'SCUZE ME!

I THINK WE'VE GIVEN THOSE ROBOTS THE SLIP-
GOOD! LET'S GET DOWN TO THE PARKING GARAGE.

DING!!

BRRR! THEY REALLY CRANK THE AIR CONDITIONING IN THESE ELEVATORS!
IT FEELS LIKE WE'RE GOING UP INSTEAD OF DOWN!

THE ELEVATOR'S TAKING A SLIGHT DETOUR ... NEXT STOP— JAIL!

HI, AIDAN, WHAT DID I MISS?
WELL, WE SOLD ALL THOSE SNOW MAKERS!
SNOW ANGEL ENTERPRISES

I NOTICE YOU'RE NOT IN COSTUME.
THE ORGANIZERS WERE SO GRATEFUL THEY GAVE US THE TABLE FREE. WHO NEEDS HALF PRICE?
SNOW AN
ENTERPR

EXCUSE ME, PLEASE— ARE YOU SNOW ANGEL?
YES—?
SNOW
ENTE

INKAWASHI-SAN! WHAT AN HONOR TO MEET YOU!
NO, IT IS I WHO HAVE HONOR!
SNOW ANGEL ENTERPRISES

WOULD YOU WANT AUTOGRAPH?
NO, NO, I WOULDN'T DREAM OF IT! I KNOW IT IS AGAINST YOUR PRINCIPLES TO SIGN YOUR NAME TO ANYTHING!

NO, IT IS I WHO WANT YOUR AUTOGRAPH!

THANK YOU, SNOW ANGEL!

PLEASED WITH OURSELVES, AREN'T WE?

NEXT DAY...
WELL, SALES ARE STILL LOUSY, BUT YOU GOTTA LOVE THE COSPLAY!
END

SNOW ANGEL

Story & Art by David Chelsea

I'M THINKING OF A NAME-
FIVE LETTERS.
IS IT AIDAN?

IT'S AFTER AIDAN, AIDAN.
IS IT ANGEL, ANGEL?

IT'S AFTER ANGEL...
IS IT ZELDA?

BEFORE ZELDA.
IS IT CARLO?

WELL, ANGEL, IS IT CARLO OR NOT?

!

STOP THE CAR!!

THERE'S A REST STOP IN FIVE MILES- CAN'T YOU WAIT?
IT'S NOT THAT!
I BET YOU ANYTHING IT'S A SNOW ANGEL THING!

WHAT IS IT?
THERE'S A DOG OFF A LEASH- THAT'S TOTALLY AGAINST THE LAW!

YES, BUT I HARDLY THINK IT'S IMPORTANT ENOUGH TO STOP THE CAR!
BUT HE'S CHASING A SQUIRREL!!
TOO BAD FOR THE SQUIRREL! SERVES HIM RIGHT- NASTY VERMIN, ANYWAY.
KILL 'EM ALL, I SAY...

BUT-BUT- IT'S A CUTE LITTLE SQUIRREL-!!!
IF YOU SAW WHAT THEY DID TO OUR APRICOTS THIS YEAR—
I HOPE THAT DOG CHEWS HIM TO DEATH- SLOWLY!

WHERE IS THIS DOG, ANYWAY?
ESTACADA.
FORGET ABOUT IT- THAT'S COMPLETELY THE OTHER DIRECTION!

ANGEL?— CARLO?
IT'S AFTER CARLO!
MAN, IT'S REALLY COMING DOWN!
IS IT GRACE?
YEAH.
MY TURN!

OK— SIX LETTERS.
IS IT MARVIN?

IT'S AFTER MARVIN!

BEER

STOP THE CAR! I REALLY HAVE TO GO!!!

WHAT IS IT THIS TIME?
ROBBERY AT A CONVENIENCE STORE!
REALLY?
WELL...SHOPLIFTING.

WE'RE NOT STOPPING FOR THAT!
WHAT, YOU THINK SHOPLIFTING IS OK?
YOU HAVE TO PICK YOUR BATTLES, ANGEL. IF WE STOP NOW, WE MAY NOT MAKE IT TO THE LAKE.

OK, AIDAN... IS IT XANDER?
IT'S BEFORE XANDER!

STOP THE CAR! I MEAN IT!!

THIS HAD BETTER BE GOOD...
SKREEEEECH!!

SLAM!

WE'LL NEVER GET THROUGH NOW!

PLOFF!

CRACK!

EVERYBODY GET IN THE CAR— AND OPEN THE SUNROOF!

WHOOSH!!

BUMP!!

WHOOOSH!!

IS IT RHODAH?

IT'S BEFORE RHODAH.
END

Story by Rebecca Celsi & David Chelsea | Art by David Chelsea | Colors by Jacob Mercy

BUT THIS – THIS WRONG WILL NEVER BE RIGHTED!

YOU'RE TAKING THIS AWFULLY SERIOUSLY-YOU KNOW THAT HE'S JUST A CHARACTER IN THE COMICS, RIGHT?
YES, YES...

UNLIKE SNOW ANGEL, WHO IS THE ONLY SUPERHERO THAT IS ACTUALLY REAL!
HMM...

HOW CAN YOU BE SO SURE?
WHAT DO YOU MEAN?

WHAT IF YOU AND I AND EVERYONE WE KNOW WERE JUST CHARACTERS IN A COMIC BOOK SOMEONE IS READING?

THAT'S THE NUTTIEST THING I EVER HEARD.
I KNOW- SOMETIMES I SAY STUFF THAT MAKES ABSOLUTELY NO SENSE!

IT'S TOO BAD THAT SNOW ANGEL IS THE ONLY SUPERHERO WHO REALLY EXISTS - AND ALSO THE LAMEST SUPERHERO EVER!
WHAT DO YOU MEAN?

THROWN-AWAY CIGARS! JAYWALKING! MISSING BIKE REFLECTORS! WHY CAN'T YOU EVER FIGHT ANY REALLY COOL CRIME?
THAT'S WHAT THE POLICE ARE FOR!

LATER THAT DAY...
BAN

FREEZE!

DON'T NOBODY MOVE AND DON'T NOBODY REACH FOR THAT DOOR! GIMME A MILLION BUCKS AND FAST!

$ OOMPAH BAN

MUNICIPAL PARK

ANOTHER SENSELESS CRIME!!

WELL, NO ONE MESSES WITH—

SNOW ANGEL!!!

FREEZE!
KEEP OFF THE GRASS

VALUABLE WORK WENT INTO THE MAINTENANCE OF THIS LAWN!

HONESTLY, SNOW ANGEL, I WAS RUNNING SO FAST I DIDN'T SEE THE SIGN!
AS IF THAT'S ANY EXCUSE!
?

GOOD WORK, SNOW ANGEL!

YOU TOOK OUT THIS DANGEROUS CRIMINAL—

AND RECLAIMED THE STOLEN MONEY!
MONEY?

YES, THE MONEY. WHERE IS IT?
WHAT MONEY? I DIDN'T SEE ANY!

ALL RIGHT! ALL SQUADS ON THE SEARCH! THE MONEY HAS NOT BEEN FOUND, THANKS TO THIS EXCUSE FOR A HERO!
BUT... I SAVED THE LAWN! I DID GOOD!

LISTEN, KID, MAYBE YOU SHOULD GO HOME, LEAVE THINGS TO US, BEFORE YOU MAKE THINGS WORSE!

BUT... I AM HELPING! AND YOU'RE WALKING ON THE GRASS!
KEEP OFF THE GRASS

INGRATES!

HI, MOM— I'M HOME!
HI, HONEY!

WAIT, MOM— YOU'RE USING THE SAME SPOON FOR STIRRING AND TASTING!!

FOR GOSH SAKES, ANGEL, IT BARELY MATTERS! AND GET OUT OF THE KITCHEN, PLEASE. I'M BUSY!

I'VE ONLY DONE GOOD ALL DAY! WHY HAS EVERYONE BEEN SO MEAN?

SNOW ANGEL!

WHO ARE YOU?
I'M YOUR GUARDIAN NORMAL KID!

I HAVE A GUARDIAN NORMAL KID? WHY?
BECAUSE YOU'RE AN ANGEL! I BESTOW ON THEE THIS ADVICE:
NK

It takes many small to hold up the great! And often, the great are hidden within the small! Trust not in the appearance of power!
GNK

Thy destiny lies in thy own hands! Art thou girl or mouse? Live for the calm before the storm, the break in the music!
WHAT THE HECK ARE YOU TALKING ABOUT?
GNK

Do the hokey-pokey! That's what it's all about! And don't forget to drink your Ovaltine!
YOU'RE CRAZY!
GN

LISTEN, I DIDN'T SAY IT WOULD BE SOUND ADVICE- JUST ADVICE!
HAVING A GUARDIAN NORMAL KID SUCKS!
GN

WHY, I OUGHTA—
WAIT- DON'T FREEZE ME! I WILL BESTOW ON THEE TRUE ADVICE!
NK

You don't miss the water till the well runs dry!

WHAT'S THAT? THAT'S EVEN WORSE THAN DRINK YOUR OVALTINE!
The truth will out, Snow Angel
GNK

HMMM....

PERHAPS THAT FIGMENT OF MY IMAGINATION WAS RIGHT- IF ANNOYING...

I'LL SHOW THEM! I'LL SEE HOW LONG THEY CAN GO WITHOUT ME! NO HELPING- NO REMINDING- NO SAVING THE WORLD ON THE SMALLEST SCALE!

THEN AGAIN, WHY WOULD I MISS THE WATER IF IT WAS STILL THERE?

NEXT DAY...
BREAKFAST, EVERYONE!

ALL RIGHT, ANGEL! I KNOW THE KNIFE AND FORK ARE ON THE WRONG SIDES OF THE PLATE! STOP GIVING ME THAT LOOK- AND DON'T YOU DARE DROP A SNOWBALL DOWN MY BACK OR WHATEVER IT IS YOU DO!

NO BIG DEAL, MOM! IT'S NOT AS IF WE'RE HAVING COMPANY OVER-

I'M GLAD YOU FINALLY SEE THINGS MY WAY, ANGEL!

GOSH, IT'S ONLY MAKING HER HAPPY!

AND THEY WERE ON THE WRONG SIDE!

COME ON, JOJO! IT'S FREEZING OUT, AND I'M MISSING THE MORNING CARTOONS!

OH NO! WELL, NO TIME TO CLEAN THAT UP, OR WE'LL MISS DANGEROUS GUY!

SUCH PETTY CARELESSNESS! I CAN BARELY RESTRAIN MYSELF FROM GIVING THEM BOTH A TASTE OF SNOWY FURY!

BUT NO— SOON THERE WILL BE CRIES OF "HELP US, SNOW ANGEL!" ONLY THEN WILL I RETURN TO RIGHTING WRONGS!
ANGEL! WHERE ARE YOU?

I'M RIGHT HERE, MOM.
OH, I THOUGHT YOU WERE OFF ON ONE OF YOUR ADVENTURES.

NO, I AM OFFICIALLY ON STRIKE UNTIL THE WORLD REALIZES HOW MUCH IT NEEDS ME!

OH, WHAT A RELIEF! I WAS WONDERING WHEN YOU WERE GOING TO GIVE THAT STUFF UP. ARE YOU GOING TO MAKE AN ANNOUNCEMENT?
THAT'S A GREAT IDEA!

SNOW ANGEL
PRESS CONF
B24 →
EINBINDER
WEDDING
← B23
SHULMAN
BAT MITZVAH
B22 →

SO - WHAT DO YOU THINK? IS SNOW ANGEL GOING TO ANNOUNCE A NEW SUPERPOWER?
MAYBE SHE'S TAKING ON A NEW SECRET IDENTITY!

MAYBE SHE'LL DECLARE WAR ON A FIENDISH SUPERVILLAIN!
OR TEAM UP WITH A CRIME-FIGHTING PARTNER!
MAYBE FIND A LOVE INTEREST!
HUSH, HERE SHE COMES-

WHERE'S SNOW ANGEL?
THAT'S HER SECRET IDENTITY, DUMMY!
SOME SECRET! EVERYBODY KNOWS!

GENTLEMEN, THIS IS MY LAST PRESS CONFERENCE. I AM RETIRING AS SNOW ANGEL, EFFECTIVE IMMEDIATELY, IN ORDER TO SPEND MORE TIME WITH MY FAMILY.

THIS DECISION IS FINAL. NO VAST WAVE OF PUBLIC OUTCRY, NO OVERWHELMING PLEA TO PROTECT SOCIETY, CAN POSSIBLY INDUCE ME TO RETURN TO FIGHTING CRIME. ARE THERE ANY QUESTIONS?
ANYONE?

I DON'T HAVE ANY QUESTIONS. DO YOU HAVE ANY QUESTIONS?
NOT ME.
SEEMS PRETTY CLEAR TO ME.

UHM— WE STILL HAVE SOME T-SHIRTS AND SNOW GLOBES FOR SALE.

ANYTHING ON THE NEWS?
WELL, THE GOVERNOR RESIGNED—
OH, AND THAT WEASEL AT THE ZOO HAD BABIES. THAT ONE'S ON ALL THE CHANNELS!

THERE'S SUPPOSED TO BE MORE SNOW THIS WEEKEND—
WELL, THAT'LL BE NICE.

HERO KID QUITS,
TOWN SHRUGS.

B-BUT, B.Z.! DANGEROUS GUY ALWAYS FIGHTS VEGETABLES! THAT'S HIS THING!
THAT'S WHY RATINGS ARE SLIPPING! WHEN'S THE LAST TIME MUTANT VEGETABLES ATTACKED ANYONE? WE HAVE TO HIT PEOPLE WHERE THEY REALLY LIVE!

GIVE ME NEW IDEAS, PEOPLE! LOOK ON THE INTERNET IF YOU HAVE TO! I WANT STORIES RIPPED FROM THE HEADLINES!

HMMM...

HERO KID QUITS, TOWN SHRUGS

TAP TAP TAP

I LOVE THIS NEW SCRIPT, JOYCE! YOU'VE GOT DANGEROUS GUY FIGHTING THINGS LIKE JAYWALKING AND NOSE PICKING THAT PEOPLE CAN REALLY RELATE TO! LET'S RUSH IT INTO PRODUCTION RIGHT AWAY!
THANKS, B.Z.!

ONE YEAR LATER...
I'VE ALREADY SEEN THIS EPISODE OF "NINJA SHARK."
LET'S SWITCH OVER TO "DANGEROUS GUY."

NOW PRESENTING— "DANGEROUS GUY, THE CARTOON!"

THIS EPISODE:
"SMALL CRIMES"

HARK! MY DANGER SENSE TELLS ME SOME BAD LITTLE BOY IS EATING PEAS WITH A KNIFE!

A QUICK LEAP INTO AN OPEN MANHOLE, AND...
HOTEL

HERE COMES— DANGER!!

MMM... PEAS!

I'LL USE MY MORPHOVISION™ TO TURN THAT KNIFE INTO A FORK!

MIND YOUR MANNERS, SONNY! DON'T EAT LIKE AN ANIMAL!

THAT WAS DANGEWOUS GUY!!

HUH! DANGEROUS GUY'S ACTING KIND OF DIFFERENT—
YEAH!

OH NO! A DOG RUNNING OFF THE LEASH AND A BABY EATING DAHLIAS IN THE PARK! WHO DO I STOP FIRST?

HE'S FIGHTING ALL THIS REALLY INSIGNICANT CRIME—
KIND OF LIKE—
CHIPS

SNOW ANGEL!
WHO'S THAT?
DM

SHE USED TO BE A SUPERHERO, LIKE DANGEROUS GUY, ONLY REAL!

SHE FOUGHT CRIMES LIKE NOT HAVING A BIKE REFLECTOR, AND WEARING WHITE SHOES AFTER LABOR DAY, AND...

... PUTTING TABLE SCRAPS IN WITH RECYCLING, AND—
SO, WHAT HAPPENED TO HER?

WELL, SHE KIND OF QUIT, BECAUSE PEOPLE DIDN'T APPRECIATE WHAT SHE DID—
WHY, THAT'S AWFUL!

WE HAVE TO GET HER TO COME BACK!

THERE SEEMS TO BE A MOB GATHERING OUTSIDE.
IS IT AN ANGRY MOB?

I DON'T THINK SO.
WELL, THAT'S GOOD.

SNOW ANGEL, COME BACK!

WE WERE WRONG NOT TO CARE ABOUT WHAT YOU DO! WE NEED A CHAMPION TO FIGHT THE LITTLE CRIMES!

HOW COME YOU FEEL LIKE THIS ALL OF A SUDDEN? WHEN I QUIT, NO ONE CARED!
IT HAS A LOT TO DO WITH THE LATEST EPISODE OF "DANGEROUS GUY," ACTUALLY!

OH, DID YOU SEE IT? WHEN HE SPEARED THAT WAD OF GUM IN MIDAIR!
THAT WAS AWESOME!
YEAH, AND WHEN HE BLEW THE LEAVES BACK IN THAT NOISY BLOWER!

THAT WAS A TOTAL TRAVESTY! DANGEROUS GUY NEVER STOOPS TO ANYTHING SO PETTY IN THE COMIC BOOKS!
OH, BE QUIET! NOBODY CARES WHAT HAPPENS IN THE COMICS!

ANYWAY, ONCE WE SAW IT ON TELEVISION, WE REALIZED - THE KIND OF THINGS SNOW ANGEL DOES ARE IMPORTANT!
AND SHE'S FOR REAL!

WELL, YOU'RE TOO LATE. I'VE BEEN TAKING MEDICATION TO SUPPRESS THE SIGNALS, AND I'M FINALLY GETTING TO ACOLYTE LEVEL IN "MINERS OF WINDSOCK"! I DON'T WANT TO COME BACK! EVERYBODY GO HOME!

GO ON, GO!
YOU HEARD HER!

THIS IS A SAD DAY- THE END OF THE COLD CRUSADER!
THE CHILLED CHAMPION!
THE SUB-ZERO HERO!
ULP- 'SCUZE ME!

NO!!

WHOOSH!

FWUMP!

EXCUSE ME– I BELIEVE YOU DROPPED THIS.

THANK YOU, SNOW ANGEL!

ANGEL?
WHAT CAN I SAY? JUST WHEN I THOUGHT I WAS OUT, THEY PULLED ME BACK IN!

AND SOON...
DON'T WALK ON THE GRASS, BRIAN! REMEMBER SNOW ANGEL!
GET A REFRESHING.
ICE CONE!
JUST LIKE SNOW ANGEL MAKES!
SNOW ANGEL SMASHES LUNCH MONEY BULLYING RING!
RAIN EXPECTED
KEEP OFF GRASS

THERE'S AN ANGEL
FIERCE AND STRONG AND BOLD—
SNOW ANGEL!

YOU WILL SEE HER
WHEN THE WEATHER'S COLD—
SNOW ANGEL!!

DROP YOUR CLOTHES
ALL OVER THE PLACE

YOU MIGHT GET SOME
SNOW IN THE FACE—

WHEN WE MESS UP,
SHE'S THE ONE WHO SCOLDS!

SNOW ANGEL!!